Guardians of Maple Hollow

Paperback: ISBN 979-8-9860716-4-0

Hardback: ISBN979-8-9860716-5-7

Ebook:ISBN 979-8-9860716-6-4

Published by Amber Chyenne

Contents

The legend of Maple Hollow

Long ago a treacherous war between; man, magic and nature broke out. This war destroyed the land and hundreds of lives were lost. The meaningless battle upset the forest spirits. In order to stop the war and keep it from repeating the spirits created three guardians. The kelpie was the first spirit; it represented nature. The next was a dryad she stood for magic. The last spirit was Uriel; he represented man. Each guardian they created took the shape of a wolf. The first one was a demon wolf, created to protect the balance. The second one stood for wisdom; it was the Shadow Wolf. The final one represented love; it was there to teach compassion to all living creatures; this was the witcher wolf. The forest spirits had hoped with their three wolves they could help bring balance back to the land but their plan failed when a demon Hunter had discovered the wolves. The guardians had fallen but this would not be the last time the three wolves would appear in history. For if chaos fell upon the land that they were placed to protect the three wolves would rise once more. When the guardians fell a council was formed to keep balance.

Chapter 1

Son Of The Exiled Spider Sage

The clan of Spider sages are shape shifting assassins. They were able to take three forms: the first one is a large spider, then they appear half human, finally the spider sage can take the form of a normal human. This group of supernatural beings are one of the members of the council. They represented humans at the table. Only a pure blood from each of the eight groups can have a spot at the table. This was the stronger child of the leader and former council member.

"She is a human! I will not have a half human in my bloodline! You will kill her or leave and I will choose someone else to take your spot when the time comes to take the council seat. Choose wisely my son." the leader of the spider sages exclaimed.

"Then choose someone else, my father. I choose my family not a seat at the council," a younger man said as he walked out of the yard.

"So be it. Don't come back then, Kumo," the leader said.

"Stay away from my family Taisho. You are no longer my father," Kumo replied, getting into a small blue car and driving off.

15 years later Kumo's son was a freshman in Maple Hollow high school unaware of his bloodline. His name is Kai, his hair is blond and he has sky blue eyes. He was 5'6", with a muscular build. His mother became a counselor for the school and his father taught the school's mythology class. As for his grandfather, he became the mayor to control the flow of information to the press. Kai often kept to himself.

"Ok class today I have a few assignments that you get to choose from. The first one is how pollution affects the environment. The next is deforestation. I expect a full report on the topic you choose by the end of the week and it must be at least 500 words. Then pictures you take yourself and where you took them. This is an easy project so if it is late I will knock off points," A teacher said, as the bell rang.

The second the bell rang the students rushed out of class.

"So Kumo, when do you intend on telling your son he is half spider sage? It would be better if he hears it from you then one of many supernaturals in this town," Cian warned.

Cian was the janitor at the school. His hair and beard is flaming red and his eyes are a deep blue. He was 4 feet tall even with a stout build.

"I do not plan to tell him. It is for his own safety," Kumo answered.

"You have even refused to teach him to fight. If you choose not to tell him for his safety then would it not make sense to train him?" Cian asked.

"Fighting is not always the answer, Cian. I must go now. I have a class waiting for me," Kumo said walking away.

"Dad, after school can I go to the library for a report for environmental science?" Kai asked, as he walked past to go to the gym.

"Yes you may but be careful and call me once you are done and I will pick you up. Are you going with a group?" Kumo replied.

"No I am not. Why would I?" Kai responded.

"It would not hurt you to talk to him about making at least one friend. He refuses to work in groups, eats by himself all the time, and does not do after school activities," the environmental science teacher said, walking up behind him.

"You can't force someone to make friends," Kumo replied, "But we know what you mean."

"I have a group project coming up in about two weeks. He will work with two other students. If he doesn't pick them to work with I will pick a group for him," the environmental science teacher said, as she walked away.

"Ok," Kumo said, walking into his classroom.

"Kai you are on my team," a boy with black hair with a red stripe in it said.

"Ok sure," Kai replied, putting his hands in his hoodie pocket and walking over to a group of boys.

"Ok now that the teams are picked you are playing dodgeball today. Remember no headshots boys. The nurse said if anyone else goes there because of dodgeball you will not be able to play it again," the coach warned.

"Yes coach. Alright let's play," a football player replied.

Most of Kai's team had been hit but the football player's team was not having much luck getting him out. He had been dodging them as though he was a ninja. After a while the coach sent them all to change before the bell rang. After class Kai was on his way to the next class when he heard something hit the lockers from the other end of the hall. When he turned around to see what it was he saw a group of boys holding another boy up against a locker.

"Hey how about you all put him down. Five against one is not a fair fight," Kai said, stepping between the boys.

"Mind your own business Kai," The leader of the boys replied.

"Yeah that is not going to happen. Leave him alone and get to class," Kai responded standing in front of the boy they were bullying.

"Last warning Kai. Get out of our way," the leader warned once more as he balled his fist.

"No," Kai replied as he dodged a punch and watched the leader's fist dent a locker.

As soon as the leader threw the first punch Kai fought back. The rest of the group stood back and watched as the two began to fight. All of the boys were too busy to notice that principal Benjamin was standing above them.

Benjamin's hair was black and his eyes were light blue. He was pale with a suit and fancy watch that allowed him to walk among the humans during the day.

"Gentleman, are you done? If so, come me to my office," Benjamin said, pulling Kai off from the other boy.

Once they made it to the office, Benjamin had the security call the two's parents.

"Ducan, your mother is sending your uncle Denali to pick you up. Kai you are to wait in the school's library until your parents are off work. Then tomorrow you will be here after school to help Cain clean the school. If you don't want to do that I will suspend you two. I am very disappointed in you both. Hopefully you learn something from this," Benjamin informed the boys.

"Hello deputy Denali, your nephew is in the office waiting for you to pick him up," the security said, pointing to the office.

Denali had black hair and blue eyes. He was 5'8" with a muscular build.

"Thank you," Denali replied, walking into the office, "Ducan you are lucky I was on break. Another fight. What were you thinking? Come on, I am dropping you off at the house and your father can deal with you."

"Yes sir," Ducan responded, glaring at Kai grabbing his bag then following his uncle out.

"Kai I know you were only standing up for another student. I will encourage that but getting into fights like you did is not how it should have been handled. You are not in as much trouble but you know how your father feels about fighting being the answer to a problem," Benjamin said, "Now go wait in the library until your parents get off."

"Yes sir. I am sorry for the trouble," Kai replied and started to walk out.

"Kai, you are not the one who bullied another student or dented the locker. You are not wrong for defending a student but for how it was handled. Fighting is not always the answer," Benjamin explained, from his desk.

Once Kai got to the library he did not waste time finding books to help with his report on how pollution affects the ecosystem. With each book he took notes from them. Then he went to the computer for more recent documentaries. After hours passed his mother met him at the door of the library.

Her name was Shiloh. She had long blond hair and gray eyes.

"Your father is staying late tonight to toture some of the students that are failing his class or need some help. Benjamin already explained what happened. I told your father I would handle it so you are off the hook. This time but don't let it happen again," Shiloh said, putting her hand on his shoulder.

"Hello there Shiloh. Where is Kumo? I need to speak to him," Taisho remarked, staring at Kai.

"Mayor Taisho, he is with students right now," Shiloh replied firmly, pulling Kai closer to her, "Now we must leave. Have a nice day."

"Ok thank you," Taisho responded walking away.

"What was that about mom?" Kai asked puzzled.

"Don't worry about it. Stay away from the mayor though," Shiloh replied walking behind him.

"Ok mom," Kai replied.

"I see you finished some of your research for your report. Did you get everything you need to write it?" Shiloh responded.

"I got most of it. I still need to take some pictures of it but the only place I can think of is the old lake next to the old power plant where those old men are always fishing at," Kai replied, looking at his phone.

"Well it is on the way home. We can stop there and you can get a few pictures. Then there is another place I will take you before we go home. Sounds good," Shloh said, starting the car.

"Yeah thank you," Kai responded.

Meanwhile Taisho walked into Kumo's class.

"Ok students, that is all for today if you still need help come talk to me tomorrow," Kumo dismissing, the students from the room.

"Hello Kumo," Taisho said from the doorway.

"What do you want Taisho?" Kumo asked.

"Why do you assume I want something?" Taisho asked, walking closer.

"Because why else would you be here? Now leave," Kumo replied.

"He doesn't know about us does he? It would be a shame if he found out. I am here to ask about some of the younger spider sages that are in the school. They say that there is a new teacher coming in a few weeks. What is his name?" Taisho responded.

"If you go near my son or wife we will have major problems. As for the new teacher, go ask the superintendent. Keep away from my family Taisho. I mean it," Kumo replied, walking past him.

"Do you really think you can keep the truth hidden from him?" Taisho asked, standing in the doorway, "This town is filled with supernaturals and magic in this town. You can't hide this from him forever Kumo. Whether you like it or not he will find out."

Chapter 2

The Black Sheep
Of The Family

"**N**estor, come on the moving van is here! We need to get going," a man yelled from up stairs.

"I am coming father," Nestor replied.

Right then a boy with brown eyes, black hair, 5'5" with a slim build came rushing down the stairs holding a box of books.

"Nestor, slow down some," Nestor's father responded, "Are all these books really needed?"

"Yes father," Nestor said as he walked out the front door.

"Ok headcount you guys. Akand I talked to the football coach. He said you can play. Hector baseball tryouts are in a week. Brek wrestling is at your new school. Joy they have volleyball and tennis so you can play both. Nestor, they don't have a science club or a robotics program. Sorry but if you want to do an after school activity you will have to see what they got," a lady with brown hair said as she counted each one of her kids.

"It is ok mother. Thank you for asking," Nestor replied, climbing in the very back of the van.

"Why are we moving to such a small town where there are no malls there?" Joy asked.

"Joy, we have been over this already. Both your mom and I got job offers from there. That and it will do you all some good," Nestor's Father answered.

"Yea Joy is right. Why can't you guys just commute to work?" Akand asked.

"Look I know none of you want to move but we think you will like it at the new place. Oh yes that reminds me here are your classes for school. Just give it a chance," Nestor's mother replied, passing out the school schedules.

"Wait, they have a class on mythology and environmental science for freshmen? These are college classes," Nestor exclaimed.

"Yes so they may not have had the after school activities but I thought you might like those classes," Nestor's father responded.

"We found a few classes that each one of you guys would enjoy," Nestor's mother said.

The next day the five kids started school. Right off the back the other four had no problem fitting in. Nestor on the other hand had a little bit of trouble.

"Hello, you must be one of the new students here. You seem a bit lost. Can I help you find your class?" Cian said, walking up behind Nestor who was looking at his schedule, "By the way I am Cian the school janitor."

"Yes thank you so much. I am looking for mythology," Nestor replied, "Oh my name is Nestor,"

"He is down that hall, third door on the left," Cian replied, then walked away.

"Thank you," Nestor said, then raced off to class.

After class Nestor stayed to ask Kumo about after school activities he could do.

"Sorry what you are telling me you don't have anything like robotics, science club or debate club," Nestor said.

"So Nestor there is not a big enough demand for those things but I will be starting a mythology after school program for a few students. So if you are interested, have your parents sign this," Kumo replied, handing him a piece of paper.

"Thank you, I guess I can give it a shot. It wouldn't hurt to give it a shot," Nestor responded, looking at the paper.

"My son will be one of the students. I think you two would get along well," Kumo said.

"Ok sure. Ummm is there any other after school activities that aren't sports?" Nestor replied.

"Here let me see your schedule. I might be able to help there are not many after school programs but some of the other teachers do after school classes for extra credit," Kumo said.

"Ok here. Thank you," Nestor replied, handing his schedule to Kumo.

"Environmental science is one of them. She has after school classes every Monday and Thursday. Talk to her and she might have a spot open for you," Kumo said, "I must go now, have a good day."

"Ok thank you," Nestor responded and raced to his next class.

When lunch came around Nestor began to look for someone to sit with. Then he saw Kai sitting by himself.

"Hey my name is Nestor. Is it ok if I sit with you?" Nestor asked.

"Why not. You are one of the new kids here right?" Kai replied, "Oh yea the name is Kai. You are in two of my classes."

"Really which ones?" Nestor asked, as he sat down.

"Mythology and environmental science. My dad is the teacher for Mythology," Kai answered.

"Oh that is cool," Nestor replied, "Hey how does every-one know I am one of the new kids?"

"Oh, this is a small town, new kids stand out. That and there are five of you," Kai replied, opening a book.

"Well I guess that makes sense." Nestor said, "What are you reading?"

"Myths and legends in the town," Kai answered.

"Cool," Nestor said, looking at the book.

Neither one knew that they were being watched.

"Seems to me as if your son might have made a friend finally,"Cian remarked.

"It seems that way," Shiloh replied, "That is one of the new students?"

"Yes he is Shiloh. He is the black sheep of the family. His siblings are all in sports with easier classes and made friends with groups quickly today," Cian answered.

"So hopefully this will be good for both of them," Shiloh replied walking down the hall.

As days passed the two boys began to hang out during and after school. From afar Taisho was watching them de-bating whether the two boys could be of use to him in the near future.

"So there is a project where we get to work in a group. Cool," Nestor said.

"Except we need a group of three. Everyone else is in groups of four and I am not keen on the idea of working with the other classmates," Kai replied.

"I hear you there. Maybe we can talk to the teacher about just working in a group of two," Nestor responded.

"Maybe," Kai said, "Well I will talk to you tomorrow."

"Ok see you later Kai," Nestor said, walking to his mom's van.

"So I see you made a friend," his mom said smiling.

"Yea," Nestor replied.

"That is good. What is his name?" she asked.

"His name is Kai. His dad teaches my mythology class and his mom is the councillor." Nestor replied, "Oh I signed up for a few after school classes this week. Is that ok?"

"That is fine, just don't over do it," Nestor's mom responded.

"Ok I wouldn't. It is only two classes and it is only next week for extra credit," Nestor said.

"Ok but you just got here, why do you need extra credit?" she asked, puzzled.

"I don't but it looks much better on me if I have the highest grades I can possibly get. That and what else I am supposed to do next week? Kai and I are going to use those classes to work on our group project for science class. The town library is closed for repairs next week so we needed to figure something out," Nestor explained.

"Ok," Nestor's mom replied.

Chapter 3

The Half Blood Witch

While the boys had become friends, a girl by the name of Tala was getting into a lot of trouble with her school and the law in L.A. Tala had golden brown hair with a bright purple highlight in it, her eyes were emerald green. She was 5'3" with a medium build. She lived with her grandmother who was a white witch. Her mother was a member of the council in Maple Hollow. The mother was a blood witch and Tala's father had no clue that she existed. He was a supernatural bounty hunter.

Tala was too busy tagging a building to notice a cop was standing behind her.

"Young lady, what do you think you are doing?" the officer asked.

"Officer Liam, what up?" Tala asked, hiding the spray paint behind her.

"Come on Tala, this again? Your school called because you skipped your classes." Officer Liam replied, "Where are you friends?"

"I would not call them friends. Considering they probably saw you and ran. So you can have your officers check the subway tunnel that is abandoned. Let me guess you are taking back to school," Tala responded, walking to the police car.

"Nope I am taking you home and we are talking to your grandmother," Officer Liam.

"Fantastic," Tala muttered.

"I don't see why you keep hanging out with those punks Tala. You are a good kid just hanging around the wrong group," Officer Liam replied.

"Who else am I supposed to hang out with?" Tala asked.

"Anyone but them," Officer Liam replied, pulling into the driveway of Tala's grandmother's house.

"What did you do this time Tala?" her grandmother asked, coming outside to meet them both at the car.

"She was tagging the buildings again," Officer Liam answered, "Mary we need to talk."

"Tala go up stairs now,"Mary ordered, glaring at Tala.

"Yes grandmother," Tala said calmly walking inside.

"Mary, I think it is time you send her to live in Maple Hollow with her aunt Nita. the longer she stays here the more trouble she gets in," Officer Liam said, "The only reason I brought her here and not the station is because she told us where to find the others. If she keeps this up she will end up in jail."

"I guess you are right. I will have her pack and have Nita pick her up this weekend so she can start school next week." Mary replied, "Thank you Liam for looking out for her."

"Don't mention it Mary," Liam said, climbing into his police car.

Once Officer Liam left Mary went back inside.

"Tala pack your stuff you are going to finish the rest of your school year out with your aunt in Maple Hollow," Mary ordered.

"What! Are you joking? I don't even know my aunt and you are telling me I am going to live with her! Do I not get a say in this?" Tala yelled outraged.

"No you don't because of your friends almost every officer knows you by name! You have been skipping school! That and one more time and they will be sending you to juvie! If that happens you will have a criminal record! That will not happen on my watch so pack your stuff!" Marry yelled back, "This is for your own good my little wolf. You will like it there and it will be good for you. If you are doing better at the end of the year you may come back if you want to."

"Ok fine," Tala replied much calmer, "Why do you call me little wolf?"

"Because I gave you the name Tala when your mother left you here when you were born. Tala in Native American means wolf. The wolf means courage, strength and loyalty. But loyalty must be earned not bought. You will learn that when you make some true friends. Your greatest strength is your compassion for others and love. There is an old Cherokee legend. There is a battle of two wolves inside all of us. One is evil. It is anger, sorrow, regret, greed, envy, lies, false pride, and ego. The other wolf is good. It is peace, joy, love, hope, humility, kindness, truth, compassion, and faith. The wolf that wins. Is the wolf you chose to feed," Mary sat on the bed by Tala and explained, "Be careful which wolf you feed Tala."

"I will grandmother," Tala said, standing up, "I guess I should start packing."

"Yes your aunt Nita will be here in two days to get you," Mary replied, walking out.

"Grandmother, thank you and I love you," Tala said, grabbing her bag.

"I love you too. And thank you for what?"

"For everything," Tala answered.

"No thanks needed my little wolf," Mary replied, "That is what family is for. Blood doesn't always mean family. Family are those who are closest to you and have your back Tala."

"I know Grandmother. You say that all the time," Tala replied.

"I know I do. This town hides secrets that can be terrifying at first but don't let that fool you. It is wonderful and magical there," Marry said and walked away.

Once the weekend ended Nita came and picked up Tala.

"You will love it there Tala and I already have your classes set up. I asked your Grandmother what you liked and went from there," Nita said as they unpacked the car.

"What classes do I have, aunt Nita?" Tala asked.

"Mythology, Environmental science, Art, P.E., Language arts. To name a few," Nita replied.

"You set up my classes?" Tala asked.

"I helped. I told the school what you liked and they showed some of the classes that you might like," Nita answered, "oh yes your grandmother said you liked to draw so I found you a sketch book."

"Thank you so much," Tala said, and gave Nita a hug.

When they walked in a large cage in the middle of the room caught Tala's attention. Then a snake slithered down some of the branches. The snake was a ball python that looked as though it was straight from the wild just with more black than normal and black eyes

"What is up with the snake aunt Nita?" Tala asked, peering around the cage.

"Who are you calling a snake, little human? I am a familiar you fool," the snake hissed.

"Aunt Nita!" Tala screamed.

"Oh yes sorry Tala I forgot your grandmother refused to tell you about our family. We come from a strong bloodline of witches. Your mother gave you up because you were half human and had no powers. Before you ask, yes Chaos did talk. He is my familiar and will go to you one day. You will have to excuse him though he is around 1,000 years old," Nita explained.

"So grandmother wasn't joking when she said this town was magical?" Tala asked, staring at Chaos.

"No she was not but you must not say anything to anyone Tala. Am I understood?" Nita answered.

"Yes I understand. Besides if I say something people might think I am crazy," Tala remarked.

"That too," Chaos said.

"That is going to take a bit to get used to," Tala replied.

The next day Tala started school and had the same classes as Kai and Nestor.

Chapter 4

Destiny Intertwines

"Kai and Nestor, this is Tala she will be joining your group," the teacher said, walking Tala over to the two.

"Umm hi," Tala said.

"Hello I am Kai and this black sheep is Nestor. Welcome to the club," Kai replied.

"Club?" Tala questioned.

"You are new here. So am I. Kai is kinda the outcast here. So yea welcome to our little club," Nestor responded.

"You are from L.A. right?" Kai asked.

"Yeah? How did you know that?" Tala questioned.

"His mom is the councilor here and someone overheard her talking to your aunt," Nestor answered.

"So what do you say rebel? You want to join our club of odd balls?" Kai asked.

"The outcast, black sheep and the rebel. Why not?" Tala replied, pulling a chair over to them.

"So what is the project?" a student asked.

"Oh yes, each group is to find soil from around the town and nearby to see how pollination affects the growth of plants and I want pictures of where the soil came from. Plus what the soil is. Feel free to mix the soils you find and make sure you are recording the growth of the plants. Here are marigold seeds," the teacher said as she gave two packs to every group, "Remember to keep everything but the soil the same. You have eight weeks for this project."

"Tala, why don't you sit with us for lunch?" Kai asked, as the three walked to Kumo's mythology class.

"Sure thing. Thanks," Tala replied walking into the class behind them.

"Awesome," Nestor responded.

"Hello you must be Tala," Kumo said, as she walked in.

"Yes sir," Tala replied, sitting at a desk by Kai and Nestor.

"Ok today we are looking at the legend that rotates around this town," Kumo announced to the class. "Can anyone tell me what the legend is about?"

"A war a thousand years ago between man, magic and nature. This war angered the forest spirits who created the three wolf guardians to end the war and to prevent another," Tala answered.

"That is correct. How did you know that you are a new student here?" Kumo asked, puzzled.

"My grandmother lived here and raised my aunt and mother here. She told me that legend all of the time. Hard to forget it," Tala replied.

"Who is your grandmother and aunt again?" Kumo asked.

"My grandmother is Mary and my aunt is Nita," Tala answered.

"Ok now I understand," Kumo relied.

"So do you know what happened to the guardians then?" Kumo asked, "Can anyone answer?"

"Yes they were discovered by a demon hunter who killed them," Kai replied.

By time lunch had come around Kai already had a few places for them to get soil from and Nestor did some research on the marigolds.

"Hey you guys," Tala said, sitting down.

"So how are you liking Maple Hollow High so far you two?" Kai asked.

"I have been here for almost two weeks now. I think it is nice for not having any after school programs like science club and robotics. I mean I already have more friends than at my old school even if it is just two," Nestor replied.

"I have to say it is a lot quieter than my old school," Tala responded, "Plus I met you two so I guess that is a plus. To moving here it beats my aunt's five foot long snake."

"So does that mean you like it here?" Kai asked.

"Yes," Tala chuckled.

"Good, hey what are you working on?" Nestor asked, grabbing Tala's sketch book.

"Oh that not much, just a few drawings," Tala answered.

"Not much. These are amazing." Kai remarked, "Is this your aunt's snake? These are marigolds, and the old power plant."

"Yea that is Chaos," Tala said, "So that was a power plant?"

"Yep, that power plant was built in the 80's and then they shut it down because there were design flaws. It killed off the fish and most of the plants near the lake because the company that had it built was out for a quick buck," Kai explained.

"That is horrible," Tala replied.

"They took out a good portion of the ecosystem without trying to fix their mistakes," Nestor responded.

"I know. The radiation levels are super low so it is safe for people to go there but plant life has not grown around there since aside from the trees that are on the outside of the radiation zone. That is why I thought we can use some of that soil for our project," Kai replied

"Yea and maybe we can figure out how to get some plants to grow there while we are at it," Tala said.

While the three were planning out the project Cian and Shiloh were watching them.

"So you have the outcast, the rebel and the black sheep. Now that is a mix," Cian remarked.

"I know it is an odd group but at least he is making friends," Shiloh replied.

"Oh yes what can go wrong when you put the half blood witch and the half blood spider sage and a human in the same group," Cian remarked.

"Ok I see your point but the two half bloods have no powers," Shiloh replied.

"Ok you got me there," Cian responded.

"Hey mom, can I walk around town with Tala and Nestor? We need to collect soil for our project," Kai asked.

"I guess but stay away from the mayor and other property and don't go in the power plant," Shiloh replied.

"Thank you," Kai said, walking back to the others.

"I see you meant our son's new friend," Kumo said, walking up behind her.

"Yes I have," Shiloh replied, with a smile.

"She is Onacona's daughter," Kumo responded.

"I know this but Onacona has nothing to do with her and we know this," Shiloh said.

"Does Onacona know she is here?" Cian asked, looking at Shiloh.

"No and it will stay like that as long as possible," Shiloh answered, "Nita asked that you guys don't say anything to her about her mother being here."

"I understand. What did Kai want to know?" Kumo asked.

"The three of them need to collect soil from around town for their project," Shiloh answered.

"Ok fine as long as they stay out of trouble," Kumo replied.

Once school let out the three made their way around town collecting soil, labeling the bags and taking pictures. After they had almost all of the soil they made their way to the power plant lake. When they got there all the plants on the edge of the lake appeared dead, the trees were almost dead and might fall over if the wind blew in the wrong direction. The lake was dark brown with green slim floating on top and two old men set on the dock fishing.

"Ok we got the soil," Nestor said.

"We have enough we can make a mixture to help a plant grow in it," Kai replied.

"Yea but what are we going to add to help a plant grow? Grandmother taught me a few ways to help a plant grow but that might not help with this soil," Tala responded.

"We might be able to mix some of them," Nestor suggested.

"Come on, it is getting late, we should get going," Kai said walking toward the road.

"Yea is there a shortcut?" Nestor asked.

"Through the woods," Kai answered.

"Is that faster?" Tala asked.

"Yea but are you two sure? You guys are not from around here and strange things happen in this town all the time," Kai responded.

"Ok so we might run into a bear, wolf, hog or cat. Have some faith it is still daylight and your house is what a mile at most," Tala replied walking to the road.

"If you two are ok with it then we can take the shortcut," Kai said.

"Then we take the shortcut," Nestor responded.

After five minutes a strange grunting sound began to follow them. Then leaves started to rustling and a twing broke behind them.

"What was that?" Nestor asked, spinning around, "umm you guys."

Standing behind them was an extremely large hog with, huge tusk. It was much larger than a normal wild boar considering it stood taller than them.

"When you said something strange is this what you ment?" Tala asked.

"I did not mean a huge hog but along those lines," Kai said, pulling both of them by the arm, "Come on we need to get out of here,"

Right then the hog began to squeal and chase them. While running the three slid down a steep hill. At the base of a hill were old runes with wiccan marlins carved in them. The runes had an old maple tree by one of them.

The other one had a beautiful lake behind it. The last one was at the base of a mountain. There seemed to be a fourth one but the only thing left was the base of the rune. The three walked into the middle of the runes and noticed the hog was unwilling to enter the runes. So each one of them began to look at each one of the runes. When they each touched a rune the runes began to glow. Then the hog ran off.

"So that was weird," Nestor said.

"Yea it was come on we need to home," Kai replied.

"I agree. Although I don't think we should tell anyone until we know what we saw. Otherwise people might think we are nuts," Tala said.

"Yea," the other two agreed.

That night Tala had drawn a picture of the hog and was working on a picture of the runes.

"What is that you are drawing, human?" Chaos asked.

"Oh that's just a large hog we saw working on a school project," Tala answered, "You know my name by the way. Please stop calling me human."

"Not that one. The one you are working on now," Chaos replied.

"Oh this is just some runes we found while collecting soil," Tala replied.

"Those are the ruins of the guardians," Nita said, walking up behind them.

"Oh so that is why the hog didn't follow us in the middle of the runes," Tala replied.

"The wild life doesn't go in the middle of the runes. They can sense the magic from them. It was smart to run to them," Nita explained.

"We didn't. We kinda rolled down a hill and landed at the edge of them. We figured the hog wouldn't follow us down the hill so we walked into the middle to get a better look at them. Then the hog showed up but seemed to be scared of them," Tala explained.

"Then what?" Chaos asked.

"Well sense it was not going anywhere and we were stuck there so we started to look at the runes. When we touched the runes they glowed and the hog ran off," Tala replied.

"Well next please be more careful Tala," Nita responded, "Now go to bed. You have school tomorrow."

"Ok good night aunt Nita. Night Chaos," Tala said, walking up stairs.

"If the runes lit up Chaos, does that mean what I think?" Nita asked.

"Indeed it does. The guardians have returned," Chaos replied, "Now the question is who is what wolf?"

Chapter 5

Demon Hunter In The School

The next day a new history teacher arrived at Maple Hollow High. he was 6'2" and was wearing black pants and a white button up shirt. His black trilby hat and trench coat was hanging by the door.

"Hello class I am your new world history teacher," the man said, "My name is Mr. Hanssen. Do you have any questions?"

The class just sat sincerely with a strong sense of unease about the new teacher.

"No questions. Then let's get started," Mr. Hanssen remarked, "Today we will be taking a look at the Battle of Lone Pine, fought between Australia and New Zealand during world war one between August sixth through the tenth of 1915."

After that Tala met up with Kai and Nestor for lunch.

"So I found a few things we can mix with the soil from the lake," Tala said.

"Good we can plant those at your house today Tala, if that is ok. Are we going to act like yesterday didn't happen?" Nestor asked.

"Yes it is ok and for now yeah. We don't want people thinking we are nuts," Tala replied.

"Tala is right, we don't want to end up in the looney bin. When we get to Tala's we can discuss what happened," Kai said.

"So we meet you and your aunt out front of the school at the end of the day,"Nestor responded.

"Tala you left this in my class during first hour. These are good but where did you see these runes? These are believed to be the runes of the Guardians," Kumo said, holding Tala's sketch book.

"We found the runes yesterday when we were collecting soil for science," Kai answered.

"Thank you sir," Tala replied, grabbing her book.

"You three found these runes yesterday? How?" Kumo asked.

"We fell down a hill," Nestor answered, "We were on our way to your house and hit a soft patch of gravel."

"At the base of the hill were the runes," Tala replied.

They made sure not to minchin the hog or that the runes glowed.

"Ok well for now on be more careful," Kumo responded.

"Ok dad," Kai said, watching him walk away.

"Shiloh, call Nita please. We need to speak with her," Kumo said, walking past.

"Sure but why?" Shiloh asked.

"The kids found the runes to the Guardians and they aren't telling the full story," Kumo replied, "If I know Nita, Tala already knows that she is a witch and more than likely told her everything."

"Maybe if you had told Kai about who his family really is, you might know what happened. I overheard them talking. They are smart and careful," Cian responded.

"So then what is it?" Shiloh asked.

"They are going to pretend yesterday did not happen while they are here because people might think they are nuts," Cian replied, "They are going to talk about it at Nita's house while they are working on the school project."

"Then call Nita then," Kumo said and walked away.

After a little bit Nita came in to talk to Kumo, Shiloh and Cian.

"Nita, did Tala talk to you about the runes in her book?" Shiloh asked.

"Yes she did," Nita replied.

"Good, what do you know?" Kumo asked.

"That they were chased there by a large hog, slid down a hill, touched the runes while waiting for the hog to leave, then the runes glowed and the hog ran away," Nita replied.

"That means," Cian responded.

"The Guardians have returned," Nita finished Cian's sentence, "Now the question is who is what wolf?"

"I think now is the point when you two tell Kai about his bloodline. Before the council figures it out," Cian said, looking at Kumo.

"I believe you are right this time we will meet you at your house Nita," Kumo replied.

"Ok see you there," Nita said leaving the room, "Who is that?"

"That is Mr. Hanssen. He is the new world history teacher," Shiloh answered.

"The marking on his watch. Is that what I think it is?" Nita asked.

"The marking of a demon hunter," Cian replied.

"I will have principal Benjamin know so he can inform the other supernaturals, know," Kumo responded.

"Ok," Nita replied and left.

At the end of the day the three met outside in the front of the building. Then they heard talking from the awning over the door. When they turned around they saw three demons playing poker.

"A suit of aces I win," one demon said.

"Ok so are we going to pretend we don't see and hear them either?" Nestor asked.

"Yep we sure are," Tala said and began to walk to Nita's car.

"Come on Nestor. Low profile, remember?" Kai replied, grabbing his arm.

"Yea I know," Nestor answered, climbing in the car.

"So you are Tala's friends. It is nice to meet you boys," Nita replied.

"Nice to meet you too Miss Nita," Nestor replied.

"It is just Nita, young man," Nita chuckled.

"Ok," Nestor said.

"Oh yeah, one more thing I might have forgotten to minchen. Chaos does not like to be called a snake," Tala warned.

"What do you mean?" Kai asked.

"You will find out when we get there," Nita replied.

"Ok sure," Nestor replied.

Once they got there they noticed a large cage in the middle of the room and Chaos was watching them as they walked in.

"So this is your aunt's snake," Nestor said, "He is big,"

"Who are you calling a snake you foolish human. I am no snake, I am a familiar," Chaos hissed.

"Nestor, did you forget what Tala told us?" Kai asked, looking at Chaos.

"I sure did. He just talked," Nestor replied.

"You got chased by a hell hog yesterday and me talking is what you are asking about," Chaos responded.

"You told him?" Kai asked.

"Ok yes I told the talking snake like familiar what happened. Who is he going to tell?" Tala asked.

"She is right, the only other one I talk in front of is Nita who also knows." Chaos responded.

"Then if you know why not ask us in the car?" Nestor asked, "I also see why your aunt knows."

"Yea she can't say we sound nuts when there is a snake familiar that talks," Kai replied.

"This is true. I did not ask you at the school because no one can know that you found those yet," Nita replied, "This town is filled with supernatural beings. A Lot of which will not like what comes with what you found but I will wait until Cian and Kai's parents get here before I say anything else. So for now go work on your project."

"Why until my parents get here?" Kai asked.

"You will soon find out," Nita answered.

"So why do I get the feeling they know more about what happened at the runes than we do," Tala said as they walked upstairs.

"You are telling me," Nestor replied, "Before I moved I would have never believed the talking snake or all this."

"I have lived here my whole life and had no clue," Kai responded.

"So why is there a new history teacher?" Tala asked, "He is the only thing in this town I get an uneasy feeling around,"

"I don't know. The last one was quiet and left in a hurry," Kai replied.

"Maybe the teacher found out about the freaky secrets the town is hiding or the hell hog ate it," Nestor remarked.

"Yea," Tala replied, "Come on we need to get these planted."

"You need to mix the soil to see if we can reverse the power plant's doing," Kai responded.

"Ok sure thing. I am not sure if any of these will work but it is worth a shot," Tala replied.

"I don't think anything will reverse the radiation in the soil for the plants to grow," Nestor said, looking at the other two.

"Have some faith, it might, it might not. What is the harm in trying right?" Tala responded with a smile.

"She has a point," Kai replied, "So what is in this mixture?"

"Oh wood ash, egg shells, shredded banana peels, coffee grounds, tea leaves, and a touch of sea salt. Hopefully with all of them the marigolds will grow," Tala answered.

"That is a long list," Nestor replied.

"I know I mixed it last night. The only thing left to do is mix it with the soil," Tala responded.

"So what about those creatures on the awning of the school?" Nestor asked.

"I think we can answer that for you," Kumo said standing in the doorway.

"Dad?" Kai turned and replied.

"Come down stairs and we will explain," Kumo responded.

Right then a snow white owl flew in through the open window of Tala's room. As it knocked off one of the plants from the desk. Tala raced across the room in a blink of an eye to catch it. When she stopped the other two looked at her in shock.

"Weren't you just on the other half of the room?" Nestor asked.

"Yea she was," Kai replied, "How did you get over here so fast?"

"I don't know," Tala answered.

"Umm ok so there is another thing to go on the list of strange things that has happened in the last two days and the owl can go on that list too," Nestor replied.

"Hey where did the owl go?" Kai asked.

"Back out the window," Nestor replied, pointing at the owl sitting on a fence post.

With the owl outside Tala raced over and closed the window, "I thought owls were nocturnal."

"They are," Nestor said, staring at it.

"Kids down stairs now," Kumo ordered.

"Ok what is going on sir?" Tala asked.

"Just go downstairs and I will explain then," Kumo said.

When they walked into the kitchen the other three adults were sitting at the table.

"Nita, Onacona's familiar just flew into Tala's room. That means she knows she is here and not with Mary," Kumo informed her.

"Wait, how do you know that was a familiar and who it belongs to? What is going on here?" Kai asked, looking around.

"I have a better question: who on earth is Onacona and why does it matter if she knows that Tala is here?" Nestor asked.

"What about the runes? Why were all of you guys so worried when you found out about us finding them? Then why did they glow?" Tala asked.

"Ok one at a time," Nita responded.

"We will start with what is going on. Starting with how your father knows about the familiar and who Onacona is," Shiloh answered.

"So what is going on then?" Kai asked.

"Ok I will start with our bloodline. We are from a long line of spider sages. The mayor is your grandfather and leader of them. He wanted me to kill your mother when he found out. When I refused he exiled me. In this town supernatural and human live in peace for now but the council has grown corrupt. Only a pure blood can take the seat for the group at the table. Now to who Onacona is. Onacona is the leader of the witches' covenant and Tala's mother. She left you with Mary because you are half human. The runes glowing means you three were picked to be the Guardians of Maple Hollow. Each one of you will be able to turn into a wolf and have abilities like Tala super speed," Kumo explained.

"So wait what?" Nestor responded, "You just made my head hurt."

"Hang on. Why is it bad that Tala's mom knows she is here?" Kai asked.

"Because the last Onacona knew Tala was in L.A. now she knows Tala is in Maple Hollow and has super speed. This means they might find out about the runes," Cian answered.

"So wait, if you guys knew my mother was here why not say anything?" Tala asked looking around, "I know she left me because I was half human Nita already explained that but no one said she was here,"

"Because it was not your mother who left you with Mary. It was me, Tala. Your mother wanted you killed," Cian replied.

"So you knew who I was to begin with?" Tala asked.

"Yes," Cain answered.

"Wait what are you if Nita is a white witch and Kumo is a spider sage and Shiloh is a human. What are you?" Nestor asked.

"Cian is a leprechaun," Nita replied.

"Wait a minute, is everyone in the school a supernatural being?" Kai asked.

"No, about a quarter of them are," Cian answered.

"Well that would have been nice to know," Kai replied.

"I know we should have told you sooner," Shiloh said, "Tala do you have any questions? You are very quiet over there."

"Yeah. If you know I am half human then you know who my father is right? I was told he doesn't even know I exist." Tala responded, "and it is nice to know that our families are abosslety nuts."

"Yea," Kai replied.

"Ummmmmmmm……… well you dad is a different story Tala," Cian replied.

"Well you said you guys would answer our questions, so," Tala responded.

"Your father is a supernatural bounty hunter," Nita answered, "and he has no clue about you and we don't know where he is."

"Well if that isn't a messed up mix. No offense Tala but aren't they like demon hunters?" Kai replied.

"No, they will not hunt a supernatural being without it becoming a threat first and they help keep us hidden," Cian answered.

"Oh well," Nestor replied.

"Ok thank you. Now what about the new teacher? He seems off," Tala replied.

"Now he is a demon hunter so you need to be extremely careful until he leaves. Tala no other questions about your dad," Shiloh responded.

"Nope. What else is there to know," Tala said.

"Wait a minute the world history teacher is a demon hunter!" Nestor yelled.

"Does no one else see a problem with this?" Kai asked.

"Yea a quarter of the school is supernatural, isn't that a problem?" Tala questioned.

"Yes it is a problem but there is nothing we can do about it right now you guys," Kumo replied.

"I can eat him. Then he will not be a problem any more," Chaos replied.

"Umm.. I don't think that will help," Nestor said, turning to Chaos, "That and you are only five foot. How will you eat him?"

"Chaos has the ability to grow up to 250 feet and shrink down to five feet. He is more than capable of eating a human," Nita answered.

"Ok then. Chaos, we do not eat people or living beings," Tala quickly replied.

"Fine I will not eat the demon hunter but how else are you going to get rid of him?" Chaos said.

"Leave that to us. You three need to learn who is what wolf and what abilities you have so you don't expose every supernatural being in Maple Hollow," Cian replied.

"Oh there is one more thing that they forgot to tell you. I was the familiar for the original Guardians. I was placed under the care of the white witches in your family Tala. That means I am you three's familiar now," Chaos explained.

"So where do we go from here?" Nestor asked.

"You three must take down the council before they cause another war," Chaos said.

"Great, how do we do that?" Tala asked.

"Yeah, Tala has a point, how," Kai replied, looking at Chaos.

"That is up to you three to decide," Chaos answered, looking at the others.

"Ok it is getting late. Nestor, we will take you home and will explain more later. You three can't tell anyone," Shiloh said, "Keep a low profile tomorrow ok,"

"Hang on. One more thing. What are the creatures playing poker on the awning of the school?" Kai asked.

"Those are low leveled demons and they are always there," Kumo replied.

"Ok then why weren't we able to see them till now?" Tala asked.

"Let me guess humans can't see low leveled demons," Nestor remarked.

"Yes that is why," Cian chuckled.

As the days passed more and more people began to go missing. The only link was that they were tied to the supernatural somehow. Meanwhile the three slowly learned how to use their new fund abilities. Within a week they figured out how to turn into a wolf.

Kai stood about 5'6" tall at the shoulders in his wolf form. His fur coat was solid black minus his markings that were flaming red and his eyes were red. From time to time flames formed around his paws. Kai was the demon wolf.

Nestor was the shadow wolf. At shoulder height he was 4'3", his fur was a light grey, his markings were blue and his eyes turned a bluish grey. Nestor always had a large shadow around him that he could jump into and come out of another one.

Then there was Tala. She was the witcher wolf. Tala was 3'6"at the shoulders but that was because she was built for speed. Her fur was a bronzen yellow and tan with purple markings. Her eyes were also purple. Tala's claws lit up purple and were able to cut through steel like a hot knife going through butter.

Chapter 6

The Next Alpha Of The Pack

A few weeks had gone by and the three had figured out how to shift, and how to use their speed or strength. Nestor figured out how to up through shadow to teleport, Kai had gotten stronger and could create fire from nothing, and Tala was able to run at speeds of 30 miles a second in human form. Then they slowly began to figure out who was what supernatural being but made sure not to say anything. It was not hard for the three to figure out who was in the dire wolf pack.

"Hey Tala, Nestor, look at the marigolds from the power plant soil mixture, they are growing. We might be able to mix that stuff in the soil by the lake to get some plants to grow," Kai said.

"Maybe," Nestor replied.

"So that is one problem solved, but we still don't know how to take the council down," Tala replied, "That and I think we might want to wait till the plant is done growing before we go and plant anything there. The plants might be toxic because there is still radiation in the soil."

"Yea lets wait for that," Nestor said, looking at the flowers.

"We can turn them against each other," Kai replied.

"That might work for a little bit but they still have the numbers and power sets on their side. Let's not forget the demon hunter," Tala reminded the other two, "and they are head figures in the town."

"What makes you so sure about that?" Kai asked.

"Think about it. Your grandfather is the mayor, the alpha to the dire wolf pack is a deputy, the superintendent is the leader of the vampires and his right hand is the principal of the high school and the demon prince is the detective. Those are all pretty high spots in the town. I bet if we keep looking we will find a very strong pattern. It only makes sense. They are in sports that control the flow of intel that comes and goes. That is why no one knows about this town's secrets," Tala explained.

"You are right," Kai replied, looking at Nestor and Tala.

"So we have to be extremely careful trying to bring the council down," Nestor responded, "We need a plan but to have a plan we have to know the enemy."

"Nestor is right, we need a plan," Tala said, "We also need to figure out who is on our side,"

"Yea how do we do that without exposing ourselves?" Kai asked.

"We watch the ones in the school starting with the dire wolf pack," Nestor replied.

"Yeah the only problem is the dire wolves in the school don't seem to like us. So how do we do that?" Kai asked.

"We know the alpha's nephew Ducan doesn't like you guys but what about his sons and daughter?" Tala asked.

"Ok," Nestor replied, "how do we get close enough to them to talk to them?"

"Nestor has a point," Kai pointed out.

"Well Owen plays football with Nestor's brother. Mateo is in our mythology class and his daughter Nora is a year younger than us but is in the same grade because of her IQ so she has our advanced classes. So maybe we can use that to our advantage," Tala explained.

"Wait, how did you know all that?" Nestor questioned.

"It was not that hard. That pack hangs out in small groups. All I did was ask a few questions," Tala said.

The next day Kai and Tala overheard some of the dire wolves talking about a plan to overthrow the council.

"Aho with all do respect your sons do not show the aggression to lead this pack and your daughter is an omega she is not able to lead the pack," a pack member said.

"True my son's may not be aggressive like Ducan but they are both much stronger than him and your children. If neither of my sons become the pack's alpha Ducan will all three of them have the ability to overthrow the council," Aho replied, "If you question me or my mate again you will be banished from this pack. We are the alphas here so do not forget your place."

"I understand Aho. How do you guys plan to overthrow the council? They have been around for a little more than a 1000 years," the pack member responded.

"We are going to expose the rest of the council members to the demon hunter," Aho answered, "I am no fool. I know that the spider sages call him here."

"Mother, why are you talking about overthrowing the council?" Nora asked, stepping out of the shadows in the library.

"That is none of your business young lady! You have no right to question me! You may be my child but you will have respect for the alphas in this pack," Aho snapped.

"Mother, if we get rid of them the town would fall into chaos. Every supernatural being would be exposed. Lives would be lost," Nora pointed out.

"Get out of my sight Nora," Aho ordered.

"Fine," Nora mumtered.

"Aho we need to choose a new alpha for the pack by the next full moon so we can start training them," Denali said as he walked in.

"I know we have five betas and three strong possibilities for Alpha. Are sons and Ducan, are the best choices so far," Aho replied.

"I will be watching all five of them. Not just those three," Denali said and walked away, "Once they have been chosen we will train them and then take the council out and the town will be ours."

Once the dire wolves left Tala and Kai called Nestor to have him meet them at Tala's.

"What on earth is it you two?" Nestor asked, looking at them.

"What happened to the books you two were sent to get?" Nita asked, walking in with Kai's parents.

"Kai, play the recording from the dire wolves in the library," Tala said.

Once the recording was done playing the adults looked shocked.

"That is not good so what is the plan?" Nestor asked.

"We talk to Nora and hope she will help. This showed that we can trust her," Kai responded.

"One low ranking wolf will not help mess with the order of the pack," Chaos pointed out.

"No but her IQ is higher than the rest of her pack and if she thinks that way maybe her brothers do too," Tala responded.

"True and her brothers are both betas. So if we can take the smartest member and take some of the stronger members from the pack we might be able to cripple them enough so they fall back in line without anyone getting hurt," Nestor replied.

Meanwhile Denali and Aho were working on picking the next alpha.

"They plan to do what?" Owen asked.

"The pack including mom and dad wish to overthrow the council. If they do, we will run an enormous chance of the entire town being exposed, not to mention all the lives that will be lost. This might start another war," Nora explained.

"Did you tell them that?" Mateo asked.

"Yes but they do not care," Nora answered.

"Then I don't know what we are going to do. Even if one of us is chosen to be the next alpha we will take the title Deta until we are old enough to take over so we will not have a say in it," Owen said.

"I know but we can't tell the rest of the council otherwise a war will break out," Nora explained, "and we have to be careful because of the demon hunter. So we need to find someone who can help."

The next morning at school Tala went up to talk to Nora.

"Hi I don't think we met but I overheard you talking to deputy Denali and a few others at the library," Tala said.

"Wh.. what all did you hear?" Nora asked out of fear.

"All of it. No worries I am not going to say a word to anyone but I think we can help each other if you are willing to listen. If so, meet me at the old power plant. I will have Nestor and Kai with me so feel free to bring your brothers," Tala said, passing Nora a piece of paper with the markings that line her arm.

"You did what?" Nestor panicked.

"Look how else was I going to get her to meet us here?" Tala asked, throwing her arms in the air, "Our best bet on them trusting us is if we are honest with them!"

"Tala is right," Owen said walking out of the woods, "So how do you know these markings?"

"First you tell us what you know about them," Nestor replied.

"They are alone," Kai said, coming up behind them, "Sorry but we had to be sure you weren't followed."

"We understand," Owen said, "These are the markings of the witcher wolf. One of three guardians stopped the war but was killed by a demon hunter. It is said that new ones will be chosen if another war was to happen."

"The question is how you know about these markings that have not been shown in any of our books or pictures. The runes have not been seen in years. So how do you know what they look like?" Mateo responded.

"Well," Tala said, then a purple mist formed around her and she shifted into her wolf form and the markings on her arm began to glow.

"Wait if she is the witcher wolf that means you two must be the other guardians!" Nora yelled.

"Sssshhhhh, Tala, are you kidding us what if they tell their pack? Chaos said not to tell anyone," Nestor panicked.

"No worries, we are wanting to stop a war. We aren't telling anyone," Owen said, "But what made you believe you can trust us?"

"Easy you three don't act like the rest of your pack and I overheard your pack in the library. Where most of your pack was willing to follow your mother and father Nora was not. So I had some faith that you two were on the same page as her," Tala said, shifting back, "So are you willing to help prevent a war before it happens?"

"Faith is not a strong tool. You know this right?" Mateo replied.

"True but my grandmother always told me a legend of two wolves inside everyone. One is evil. It is anger, sorrow, regret, greed, envy, lies, false pride, and ego. The other wolf is good. It is peace, joy, love, hope, humility, kindness, truth, compassion, and faith. The wolf that wins. Is the wolf you chose to feed," Tala said, "We all must be careful what wolf we chose to feed. So will you help us or not."

"Yes but we do not want our pack harmed unless it is absolutely needed," Mateo responded.

"That is why we want your help. We want to avoid as much bloodshed as possible. We also must be careful on how we take down the council because they hold high spots in the town. One wrong move and we might end up exposing every supernatural being in the town," Kai replied.

"In order to do so we must team up with others that can help dismantle the council without killing anyone. We will have to work with others that are not wolves. Are you still going to help us?" Tala added.

"Yes we will help," Owen said.

"Thank you," Nestor said.

As the six went through the woods to get to town they noticed some of the dire wolves were stalking the edge of a lake with a weeping willow. In the middle of the lake a woman's head barely sat above the water. Only her eyes and nose were visible.

"What are they doing?" Tala asked.

"What is in the lake? Why are they stalking the woman?" Kai asked.

"This lake is where the mermaids live. They can only leave the lake during a harvest moon but why are they stalking the lake I have no clue. This is not our territory so they should not be hunting here at all," Owen answered.

"Mother more than likely sent them. They are the only group that can't enter town every day. It would make the most sense for the pack to attack them first," Nora replied.

"That's right. What do we do?" Nestor asked.

"Wait, that is our father and Ducan leading the attack," Mateo said.

"So what is the plan? We are outnumbered. There are ten of them and they are really strong," Nora replied.

"True but there are six of us and three of us have powers. We are in this together. That is what a pack is for right?" Tala said, "We can't let them kill the mermaids."

"Are you sure about this?" Nestor asked.

"I agree with Tala. We know how to use our powers for the most part and someone has to stop them," Kai said, "We are supposed to keep balance between man, magic and nature."

"Really you will help?" Nora asked.

"Ummm… If we are going to do something now because mother just showed up," Mateo added.

"What do you say Nestor are you in?" Kai asked.

"Ok might as well they will find out about us eventually right. I guess it is time to make a stand now," Nestor replied, turning into a wolf.

"You can wait here if you want," Tala said, turning to the other three before shifting into a wolf.

"We are a pack right?" Owen said, shifting into a black wolf.

"Alright then come on," Kai said, shifting and racing toward the lake.

"Back off now!" Tala warned, stepping between Aho and the lake.

"What is a runt like you doing here? Stand down I am the Alpha so obey me," Aho growled.

"I don't take orders from you. I am not of your pack. I am the witcher wolf," Tala snapped, unwilling to move.

"What do you take me as a fool," Aho laughed.

"I don't think that is funny, what are you guys doing here?" Owen asked.

"My son put this wolf in her place," Denali ordered.

"She is not a pack member, she is a guardian and so are the other two. So why are you here?" Mateo replied, walking up beside the other four.

"Just taking out the splash of mermaids. Then blame it on shapeshifters. Now move out of our way and help us," Denali barked at Owen and Mateo.

"No father! This is wrong and will cause another war," Nora snapped.

"You know the punishment. If you do not move you all will be banished from the pack," Aho warned.

The three turned to Tala, Kai,and Nestor to see what to do.

"Which wolf will you feed?" Tala asked, "I do not expect you to turn your backs on them but ask yourselves what do you think is the right thing to do."

"We will not let you kill the mermaids. Causing this fight will expose every supernatural in town, cost lives of who knows how many people and create another war. So banish me if you want but you will not kill the mermaids," Owen said, stepping closer to the guardians.

"Owen is right. The cost for the power you seek is too high. Innocent lives will be lost because of it," Tala pleaded.

"Banish me if you wish but I know what the cost will be and I can't sit by and follow blindly as you start a war to gain power," Nora said, remaining put with her head held high.

"I will leave the pack in that case. What you are doing is wrong and we want no part of it," Mateo replied.

"You fools! There are six of you and eleven of us. You don't stand a chance," Ducan laughed.

"That may be true but three of us have powers. Is that a fight you wish to pick Ducan?" Kai asked.

"How did you know my name?" Ducan asked, puzzled.

"That part does not matter, does it. Three of us are the guardians that means your pack knows that we have powers. So they know numbers do not matter right now. So we ask again, are you sure this is a fight you want to pick?" Nestor asked.

"Fine so be it. Mateo, Owen and Nore do not enter our territory again. Ducan you are the next alpha," Denali growled, "Move out now!"

"Thank you," Tala said, walking up to the three, "I know that must have been hard."

"Thanks Tala. you three were right we have to stop this war," Owen replied, watching his parents pack walk away, "Now we need to find a place to live,"

"I think we can help with that," Kai said.

"After all we are a pack right?" Nestor asked.

"Yeah, thank you guys," Mateo and Nora replied.

Chapter 7

Fresh Start

"Thank you so much for letting us stay here," Owen said.

"You can stay here until we can get a hold of an old friend. After all you are pack members of my niece and there are three other rooms," Nita said, showing each of them their rooms.

"Wait you are Onacona's sister," Nora responded.

"Yes I am. No worries, I have nothing to do with her," Nita replied.

"That means you have a spot at the council," Mateo implied, turning to Tala.

"Ummm… I think you forgot a rule to take a seat at the council. The one in line must be pure blood," Tala replied, "My grandmother raised me for a reason."

"So you are half human?" Nora asked.

"Well yea," Tala replied.

"So it seems that we all have a lot more in common than it seems," Owen replied, looking at Tala, "We already knew about who Kai's family was. Plus the three of us are banished from the pack and it seems like your family didn't want you there for your safety."

"Ummm….. Dude not exactly. Tala's dad is a bounty hunter who does not know she exists. Then her mother wanted her dead when she was born. If it was not for Cian she would be dead," Kai explained.

"Oh sorry," Owen said quickly.

"Don't be if I would have been a full blooded witch I would have been raised by a psychopath lunatic. Then we would definitely have a war. So don't be sorry," Tala replied.

"Nice way to look at things," Nora responded.

Later that day Tala went to water the marigolds and saw the one with the soil mixture had bloomed with a head like flower that had teeth and they all glowed in the dark. The marigold began to snap at her in hunger.

"Aunt Nita!" Tala yelled.

"Tala, why are you yelling?" Owen asked, "Ummmm!!! Nevermind! Nita!"

"I am coming!" Nita replied coming down the hall, "Now what seems to be the problem?"

"Our science project is trying to eat me. I don't think this is what the teacher meant," Tala said.

"I don't think you should bring that one to school. You have five others without heads that will not try to eat anyone that walks past it," Owen pointed out.

"Owen is right," Nita responded.

"Ok what do I do with this plant," Tala asked, "Feed it?"

"You can keep it or kill it. That is up to you but if you keep it, get a bigger pot for it and one that it is not going to break. Oh when you go to school be sure to tell Nestor and Kai not to use the soil mixture anywhere near the powerplant. The town has plenty of problems as it stands now. We don't need to add man eating plants to it," Nita answered.

"Wait! What the hell am I going to feed it?" Tala asked, turning to the marigold that was still snapping at them.

"There is some meat in the fridge that is about to go bad, give it some of that for now," Nita replied.

The next day Owen, Mateo and Nora sat with Kai, Nestor and Tala.

"Wait so the plant has a head and eats meat now?" Nestor asked.

"Yes and try to eat anything that walks past it. That reminds me I have to get a bigger pot for it after school," Tala replied.

"Well so much for the plan on getting the plants to grow near the powerplant. Unless we want man eating plants," Kai chuckled.

"Yea," Mateo laughed.

"Please don't," Nora jumped in.

"Relax, we will not do that. We just wanted to see if we could get the wildlife to grow by the powerplant again. We will not do anything to the powerplant knowing the plants will eat meat and glow in the dark," Kai replied.

"Well well looky what we have here. The outcasts hanging out with the mutts," Ducan snorted.

"We may be mutts and outcasts but at least we aren't arrogant puppets," Tala replied, glancing behind her.

"What did you just call me?" Ducan asked with rage filling his eyes.

"I called you a puppet," Tala said, without moving an inch.

"Listen here you mutt I know you three are the guardians so if I was you I would watch my step because you are outnumbered," Ducan snapped.

"Why should we fear a glorified beta? That is all a deta is right? Then the pack might outnumber us but we know you don't give the orders. That is the two alphas that give the order," Tala replied, "I've seen cats with more bite than you, Ducan. You might as well be a puppy to those cats."

"What did you just call me?" Ducan snapped once more.

"You heard her, Ducan, you are only a glorified beta and a puppy," Owen said looking up.

"Whatever you mutts," Ducan said, walking away.

"Thanks for sticking up for us," Mateo said.

"Hey we are a pack now if they mess with one of us they get us all," Tala replied.

"Yea," Kai jumped in, leaning on Mateo's shoulder.

After school they went to Tala's house to see the man eating marigold. That was still snapping at everything that moved.

"So the talking snake was one thing but I think your man eating flower is a whole new ballpark," Mateo said looking at the marigold from the doorway.

"Who are you calling a snake, little human? I am a familiar, you fool." Chaos hissed, slithering down the hall.

"I am not a human. I'm a dire wolf," Mateo said, turning his head to Chaos.

"But you look like a human. I am a snake because I look like one that means you are a human because you look like one," Chaos hissed.

"Ok I see the point. I am sorry but you know you can't talk in front of normal humans right?" Mateo replied.

"I know this but you are not a human and neither are they," Chaos replied, "So I expect you six not to call me a snake in this house,"

"We understand Chaos," Nora responded.

"Thank you Nora," Chaos replied, "Please switch that flower to a bigger pot before that one breaks."

"Working on that Chaos," Kai replied.

"Give that plant normal potting soil please. We do not need it getting any bigger," Owen pleated.

"Will do Owen," Tala said, moving the marigold to the bigger pot, "Lucky we used biodegradable pot for them."

"Yea, nice call on the pots, Nestor," Kai replied.

"It is nice to see all of you guys are getting along." Kumo said, stepping in the doorway.

"You six make a good pack but you still need to get others on your side. So what is your next play for the board," Cian said, looking at them.

"Well we don't know the other groups aren't as easy," Tala replied.

"I think we can take a weekend and enjoy a win," Nestor replied.

"That is a good idea but can I make a suggestion?" Nita asked.

"Sure what is the idea," Kai asked.

"Don't just look at the members of the council and their groups. This town has a lot more magic in it then just you kids and them," Nita pointed out.

"Thanks," Tala replied, "So what others are in the town?"

"I guess we will find out," Nora responded.

Over the weekend the six began to figure out how to find other creatures in the town. They had found out that the museum had records of what mythical creatures that live in the town.

"So we can talk to the museum keeper to see the books and scripts to find out what supernatural beings are living in the town or what creatures did live here," Nestor said.

"Yea, it might not be much but worth a try," Kai and Mateo replied.

"We have to have some faith. The fate of the balance is setting on our shoulders. We only fail if we give up," Tala responded.

"Tala is right. The odds may not be in our favor at the moment but we have to change that ourselves," Nora pointed out.

"We all got a fresh start here, let's not waste it," Owen said, looking at the other five.

With that the guardians became more than just three lone wolves, they became a pack. This time the guardians were not alone in this fight to keep the balance. Can these guardians keep the balance where their predecessors failed or is history doomed to repeat itself?

* 9 7 9 8 9 8 6 0 7 1 6 4 0 *